SPACE

Jennifer Daniel

Researched by
Simon Rogers

B P P

SPACE

Jennifer Daniel

INTRODUCTION

Space is so mind-bogglingly vast, with distances so huge, that it's hard to begin to understand it. The planet we live on is just a tiny speck, located in a solar system in a galaxy that is one of billions of galaxies within the Universe. There is still so much to learn, and many questions remain unanswered; all astronomers, physicists and other scientists can do is use the evidence they glean to try to fathom the mysteries of space.

The invention of the telescope has allowed us to explore the outer reaches of space from Earth. We understand that galaxies are filled with stars, planets, dust and gas, held in place by gravitational force and that the planets in our solar system orbit the Sun. And we understand that without the Sun, we would not be able to exist.

As far as we know, Earth is the only planet in the Universe to sustain life – but as yet, the Moon is the only planetary body that humankind has stepped foot on besides our own. Ever-advancing technology has allowed us to travel and look further and further into space to observe and explore.

This book unravels some of the mysteries of space with amazing information graphics. Turn the page to understand the facts and bring our Universe to life at the speed of light...

THE UNIVERSE

Once, there was nothing. So how did the Universe as we know it come to be? The Big Bang is thought to have been the simultaneous creation of space, time, matter and the Universe. Millions of years after the Big Bang, stars began to form, and billions of years after that, galaxies and planets. Scientists deduce that the Universe is nearly 14 billion years old.

Across the Universe, there are billions of galaxies, one of which is the Milky Way. The Milky Way is in turn made up of hundreds of solar systems, and at the centre of one of these systems is our Sun. Orbiting the Sun are eight known planets, and we live on one of these – Earth. We are just a tiny dot in a Universe so big that scientists can only guess at its size.

Measuring the Universe appears impossible, but we can use a unit of vast distances, the light year, to understand the expanse of space.

This chapter looks at the Universe: what it is, where we are situated in it, and how it began and has evolved.

THE BIG BANG

Scientists believe that the Universe began with
an explosion called the Big Bang nearly 14 billion
years ago. Before the birth of the Universe,
time, space and matter did not exist.
Here is a timeline showing
briefly the sequence of events.

Before this point, time does not exist.

The Universe is a bubble smaller than a pinhead.

It is incomprehensibly hot, dense and unstable.

AFTER 1 SECOND

OFF WITH A BANG

The Universe suddenly
bursts and time begins.
The Universe expands
to the size of a galaxy,
and continues to grow
at a fantastic rate.

WHAT'S THE MATTER?

Matter, and its
opposite, antimatter,
are created. Much
of the antimatter
cancels out the matter,
destroying it, but
some survives.

POSITIVES AND NEGATIVES

Quarks – subatomic
particles carrying a
positive or negative
charge – begin to take
shape and form protons
and neutrons.

GOOD COMBINATION

Protons and neutrons
combine to form
nuclei, the core of
atoms.

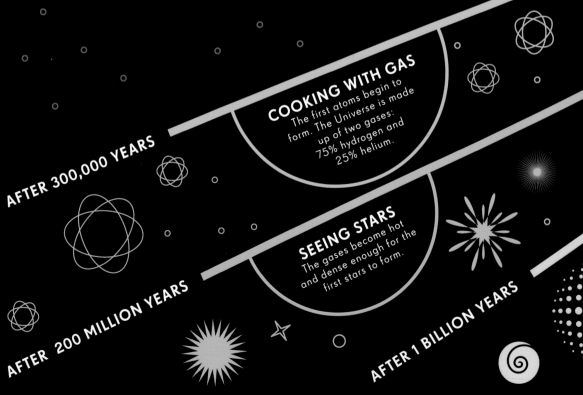

COOKING WITH GAS

The first atoms begin to
form. The Universe is made
up of two gases:
75% hydrogen and
25% helium.

SEEING STARS

The gases become hot
and dense enough for the
first stars to form.

AFTER 300,000 YEARS

AFTER 200 MILLION YEARS

AFTER 1 BILLION YEARS

DARK SIDE

The expansion of the Universe speeds up thanks to dark energy.

HERE AND NOW

data we deduce from the most accurate collected that the Universe is 13.8 billion years old.

ORBIT

WHERE DOES EARTH SIT IN SPACE?

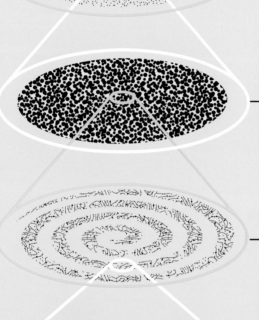

THE UNIVERSE

The Universe encompasses the entirety of everything that we know exists. We don't know how big the Universe is, or even if ours is the only one!

LOCAL GALACTIC GROUP

Also known as the Local Group, this cluster is formed of approximately 54 galaxies and dwarf galaxies, each located within 5 million light years of our own galaxy, the Milky Way.

MILKY WAY GALAXY

Our solar system is situated within the Milky Way galaxy. The Milky Way is around 100,000 light years across and contains hundreds of billions of stars, including our Sun.

SOLAR SYSTEM

Earth is located in the solar system, which encompasses everything that orbits the Sun. The solar system's boundaries are not clearly defined but are no more than 2 light years from the Sun.

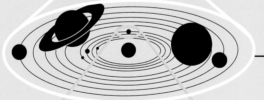

EARTH

Earth is our home planet, and is the only one known to support life. It is the third planet from the Sun, and the densest planet in the solar system.

JET SET
The galaxies are moving further apart as the space between them expands.

HOW BIG IS THE UNIVERSE?

THE SKY'S THE LIMIT

Scientists determine how many galaxies there are in the Universe by counting the number in a small area of sky...

No one knows the exact size of the Universe, but it is incredibly huge. We don't even know if it has an edge. We can only see out to a distance of about 14 billion light years from Earth.

1 PERSON

24.5 GALAXIES

...and using this data to estimate the total number that might exist.

PERSONAL SPACE

It has been estimated that there could be 170 billion galaxies in the Universe. This would mean that there are 24.5 galaxies in space for every single person on Earth.

It would take a modern fighter jet more than a million years to reach the star nearest to the Sun.

HOW DO WE MEASURE SPACE?

Distances in space are so vast that they are measured in terms of the distance that light can travel in a certain time.

SPEED OF LIGHT

Light travels at 671 million miles an hour. That is fast enough to travel around Earth 8 times in one second.

GUIDING LIGHT

A **light year** is the distance that light can travel in a vacuum in one year.

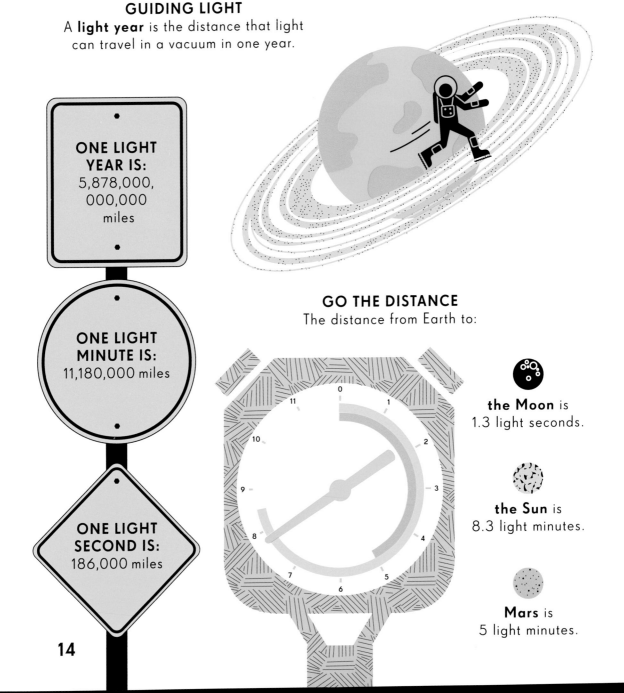

ONE LIGHT YEAR IS:
5,878,000,
000,000
miles

ONE LIGHT MINUTE IS:
11,180,000 miles

ONE LIGHT SECOND IS:
186,000 miles

GO THE DISTANCE
The distance from Earth to:

the Moon is
1.3 light seconds.

the Sun is
8.3 light minutes.

Mars is
5 light minutes.

EVERYTHING IS RELATIVE

One of the most important discoveries of the 20th century was made by Albert Einstein. He understood that matter and energy are two forms of the same thing.

This means that matter can be changed into energy and back again, as shown by the equation $E=mc^2$.

$$E=mc^2$$

E = energy   **m** = mass   **c** = the speed of light

Einstein's theory assumes that the speed of light is constant.

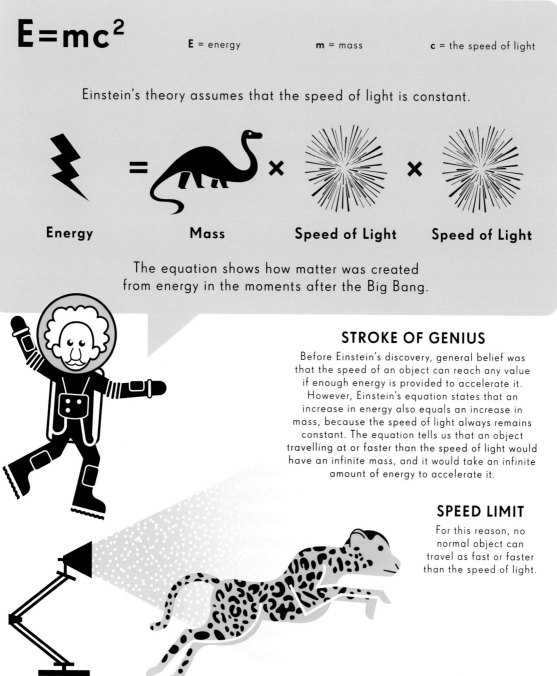

Energy   **Mass**   **Speed of Light**   **Speed of Light**

The equation shows how matter was created from energy in the moments after the Big Bang.

STROKE OF GENIUS

Before Einstein's discovery, general belief was that the speed of an object can reach any value if enough energy is provided to accelerate it. However, Einstein's equation states that an increase in energy also equals an increase in mass, because the speed of light always remains constant. The equation tells us that an object travelling at or faster than the speed of light would have an infinite mass, and it would take an infinite amount of energy to accelerate it.

SPEED LIMIT

For this reason, no normal object can travel as fast or faster than the speed of light.

WHAT IS THE UNIVERSE MADE UP OF?

The entire Universe is composed of matter and energy. Ordinary matter, made up of atoms, is everything we can sense, measure or detect. There are also energies that can be detected and measured on the electromagnetic spectrum. But 95 per cent of the Universe is made up of dark matter and dark energy that cannot be detected at all with current scientific instruments!

THE ELECTROMAGNETIC SPECTRUM

Electromagnetic waves transmit energy, and are classified according to their frequency; the shorter the wavelength, the higher the wave's energy. Different types of waves have different uses in our everyday lives.

High Frequer

Visi

Visible rays are broken down into the 7 colours of the rainbow. Each colour has a differ wavelength

Low Frequency

Infrared

Microwaves

Radio Waves

Radio waves have the longest wavelengths.

With the shortest wavelength, gamma rays are generated by the hottest regions of the Universe. They are emitted in violent events like supernova explosions.

DARK MATTER

Scientists theorize that dark matter must exist in order to explain the behaviour of galaxies, which act as though some invisible matter is exerting a gravitational force.

No one knows what dark matter is made of. It is invisible – it does not absorb, emit or reflect light.

ORDINARY MATTER

Also known as normal or atomic matter, ordinary matter accounts for just a tiny slice of the Universe!

Dark energy: 71.4%

Dark matter: 24%

DARK ENERGY

Scientists speculate that almost three quarters of the Universe is filled with dark energy. They are unable to detect it, but they hypothesize that it repels gravity, and is responsible for the increasingly fast expansion of the Universe.

Ordinary matter: 4.6%

17

GALAXIES AND STARS

The Universe is made up of billions of galaxies, which are systems filled with stars, planets, dust and gas, held in place by gravitational forces. Galaxies come in all sorts of shapes and sizes, and are thought to have a supermassive black hole at their centre.

Our own galaxy, the Milky Way, is known as a spiral galaxy – it has spiralling arms or tendrils of stars formed as the galaxy spins. There are also irregular galaxies, made from two galaxies colliding, and others that are cylindrical.

Stars come in different shapes and sizes too, and are created in different ways. They have their own life cycle; born as nebulas, building up gases and heat, and becoming either red giants or supergiants, which cool into white, then black, dwarfs, or explode before fading. Sometimes a star will collapse earlier in its life cycle, and scientists believe this creates an extremely dense mass called a black hole, the gravitational pull of which is so strong that nothing can avoid it.

Let's see if you can uncover some of the secrets of the skies...

GALAXIES BIG AND SMALL

Galaxies are systems filled with stars, planets, dust and gas. They come in all different shapes and sizes.

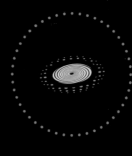

NGC 7049

NGC 7049 has qualities of both spiral and elliptical galaxies, with a rope-like dust ring.
Distance: 100 million light years from Earth
Diameter: 150,000 light years across

THE MILKY WAY
Diameter: 100,000 light years across

EARTH
You are here.

INTERGALACTIC RIDE

It is estimated that the Universe might contain as many as 170 billion (170 thousand million) galaxies. Here is a quick tour of some other galaxies outside of our own.

RAISING THE BAR

Two-thirds of all spiral galaxies, including the Milky Way, have a central bar formed of stars. These are called barred spiral galaxies.

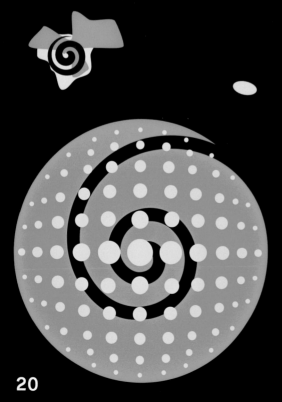

CARTWHEEL GALAXY

The Cartwheel galaxy was once a spiral galaxy. It is now irregularly shaped with a bright ring.
Distance: 500 million light years from Earth
Diameter: 150,000 light years across

ALL SHAPES AND SIZES

Galaxies come in wildly different sizes. Some giant elliptical galaxies may have up to 100 times the mass of our galaxy, which equates to 1,900 trillion suns. Others, like the ultra-compact dwarf galaxies (that scientists have just discovered), may have just a few tens of millions of stars. Our galaxy, the Milky Way, is a dwarf galaxy.

SHAPING UP

Galaxies are classified according to their shape. Over time, they can transition from one kind to another.

ELLIPTICAL GALAXIES

Elliptical galaxies usually have no spiralling arms and are round, cylindrical, or oval. They tend to be filled with very old red and yellow stars, and contain little dust or gas.

SPIRAL GALAXIES

Spiral galaxies are disk-shaped, with spiralling arms made up of stars, gas and dust. The arms are formed as the galaxy spins. Many galaxies start out as spiral before transitioning into a different shape.

IRREGULAR GALAXIES

These galaxies have no particular shape. They contain a lot of gas, dust and hot blue stars. They are usually formed by one galaxy colliding with another.

DARK HEART

Every galaxy has one supermassive black hole at its centre, and millions of smaller stellar black holes. The bigger the galaxy, the bigger the size of its supermassive black hole.

MALIN 1

Malin 1 is one of the largest known spiral galaxies. **Distance**: 1.1 billion light years from Earth **Diameter**: 650,000 light years across

21

THE MILKY WAY

Our solar system is part of a galaxy called the Milky Way, which was born more than 10 billion years ago. It is a spiral, disk-shaped galaxy, 100,000 light years across, and up to 2,000 light years thick.

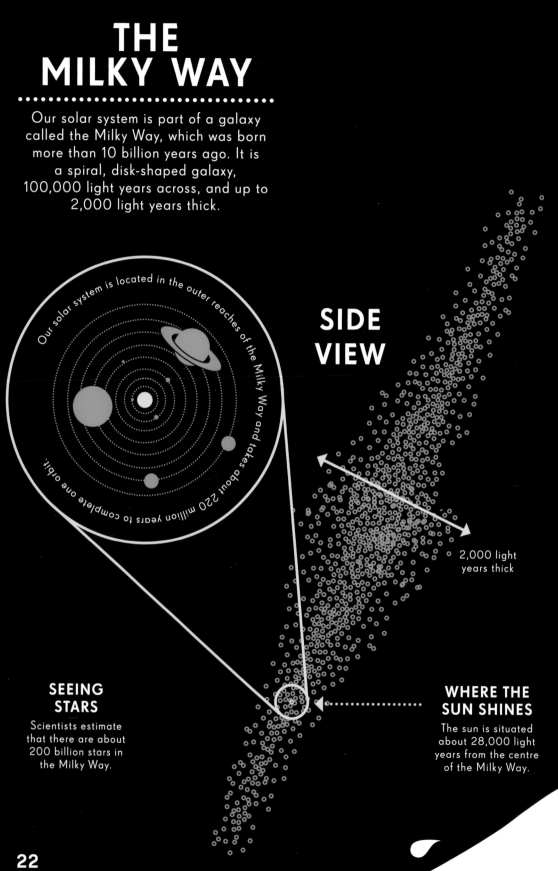

Our solar system is located in the outer reaches of the Milky Way and takes about 220 million years to complete one orbit.

SIDE VIEW

2,000 light years thick

SEEING STARS

Scientists estimate that there are about 200 billion stars in the Milky Way.

WHERE THE SUN SHINES

The sun is situated about 28,000 light years from the centre of the Milky Way.

GATHERING DUST

It has been impossible for astronomers to observe the very centre of the Milky Way because it is blocked from view by clouds of gas and dust.

CENTREPIECE

Most scientists agree there must be a supermassive black hole at the galaxy's heart.

100,000 light years wide

TOP VIEW

Our Sun

A STAR IS BORN...

Scientists estimate that there are at least 70 sextillion (70 thousand million million million) stars in the Universe. All stars have a life cycle, from formation and evolution to collapse.

NEBULA

Stars are born in a cloud known as a nebula, made up of dust and hydrogen and helium gases. As the cloud shrinks, smaller, dense masses form and begin to spin. These masses heat up, and when they reach 10 million°C, nuclear reactions begin which form a star.

RED SUPERGIANT

Stars with a mass at least eight times more than that of our Sun form a red supergiant.

STAR

As the star burns through its hydrogen fuel, it produces light and heat. Our Sun is an average-size yellow star, or yellow dwarf. Stars smaller and cooler than the Sun appear red, while larger, hotter stars appear blue.

RED GIANT

Towards the end of its life the star runs out of hydrogen fuel. Its core heats up, which causes the star to expand and its outer layers to collapse. This is the star's red giant phase.

AND DIES...

SUPERNOVA

A red supergiant can last only a few million years before its instability causes it to blow apart in a dramatic explosion called a supernova. For a week or so, the supernova burns brighter than any star in the galaxy before quickly fading.

NEUTRON STARS

Sometimes a supernova collapses back on itself to form a tiny, incredibly dense neutron star. Neutron stars have an average diameter of only 12.5 miles/ 20 kilometres. Some neutron stars, known as pulsars, spin rapidly and pulsate light. Pulsars lose their energy over time and become normal neutron stars.

BLACK HOLE

Scientists think that sometimes a supermassive red giant collapses to form a black hole, a mass so dense that nothing – not even light – can escape its gravitational pull.

WHITE DWARF

When the red giant stabilizes, it sheds its outer layers, forming a cloud known as a planetary nebula. The old star cools, shrinks and becomes a small, dense, dim white dwarf.

BLACK DWARF

Billions of years later, once the white dwarf has completely cooled, it becomes a cold dark mass, invisible to the eye, known as a black dwarf.

WHAT IS A BLACK HOLE?

Black holes cannot be seen because not even light can escape their gravitational pull, but there is scientific evidence of their existence.

OUTER HORIZON

In this area, the gravitational pull is weak enough for passing matter to escape. If a black hole were a waterfall and you were swimming in the river, from here, you would still be able to swim upstream.

EVENT HORIZON

This is the point of no return, similar to a waterfall's edge, from where it is impossible to swim away. Here, gravity causes space to fall in on itself faster than the speed of light, which is why light cannot escape it.

THE SINGULARITY

All of the matter that falls into the centre of a black hole forms a point smaller than an atom, called the singularity. Here, gravity is at its strongest. Current theories don't allow scientists to fully understand this part of a black hole.

OUTER HORIZON

Light escapes

Light is stationary

EVENT HORIZON

THE SINGULARITY

Light is pulled in

HIDDEN TALENT Black holes are invisible and therefore impossible to see, but their effect on the gas and dust around them can be seen. Every galaxy has one supermassive black hole at its centre, and millions of smaller stellar black holes. The bigger the galaxy, the bigger its black hole.

DARK THOUGHTS Albert Einstein theorized that black holes are created when a huge star collapses in on itself to create an incredibly dense mass in an area smaller than one atom.

LIGHTS OUT Black holes are regions of space with such strong gravitational pull that nothing, not even light, can escape them. They are nature's most destructive force.

SPAGHETTI-OH Anything sucked into a black hole would experience a gravitational pull so strong that it would be stretched into a long, thin shape and eventually crushed. Scientists call this process spaghettification.

THE SOLAR SYSTEM

The part of the Universe we know the most about is the solar system that we live in. Orbiting around our star, the Sun, are eight planets: Mercury, Venus, Earth, Mars, Jupiter, Saturn, Uranus and Neptune. The solar system is also made up of hundreds of other planetary objects that orbit the Sun in the same way.

As well as the main planets that we know well, there are five known smaller, or dwarf, planets. Scientists think there are probably hundreds more dwarf planets that we have yet to discover. In amongst all these dwarf planets are comets – ice-covered objects that fly through space and can sometimes be seen from Earth with our own eyes.

Scientists have been able to study many elements of the solar system – comets, asteroids and meteors – by sending robots, satellites, and even people into space.

This chapter delves deeper into the mysteries of our solar system.

OUR SOLAR SYSTEM

Our solar system contains:

1 star
Our Sun is the star around which everything in the solar system orbits. The first person to prove this was the 'father of modern science', Italian astronomer Galileo Galilei, who was born in 1564.

Mercury

Venus

Earth

3,246 known comets
Often called 'dirty snowballs', these ice-coated objects are left over from the birth of our solar system and are thought to have brought water to Earth.

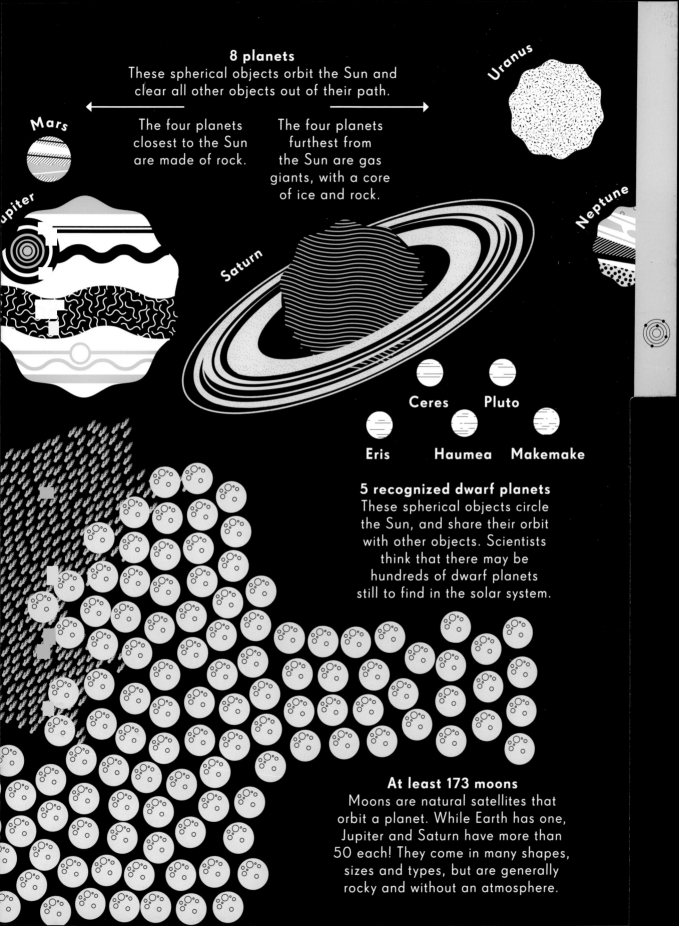

8 planets
These spherical objects orbit the Sun and clear all other objects out of their path.

The four planets closest to the Sun are made of rock.

The four planets furthest from the Sun are gas giants, with a core of ice and rock.

Uranus

Mars

Jupiter

Neptune

Saturn

Ceres   Pluto

Eris   Haumea   Makemake

5 recognized dwarf planets
These spherical objects circle the Sun, and share their orbit with other objects. Scientists think that there may be hundreds of dwarf planets still to find in the solar system.

At least 173 moons
Moons are natural satellites that orbit a planet. While Earth has one, Jupiter and Saturn have more than 50 each! They come in many shapes, sizes and types, but are generally rocky and without an atmosphere.

ALL THE PLANETS IN THE SOLAR SYSTEM

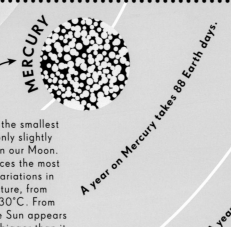

MERCURY

Mercury is the smallest planet – only slightly bigger than our Moon. It experiences the most extreme variations in temperature, from 180°C–430°C. From Mercury, the Sun appears three times bigger than it does from Earth.

A year on Mercury takes 88 Earth days.

A year on Venus takes 225 Earth days. It takes Venus longer to rotate once around its axis than it takes to circle once around the Sun.

EARTH

Earth is the only planet known to sustain life. About 71% of its surface is covered in water. Its atmosphere protects it from in-coming asteroids and is the only one that is breathable. It has one moon.

VENUS

Unlike Earth, Venus spins clockwise, so the Sun rises in the west and sets in the east. It rotates very slowly: one day on Venus is the equivalent of 243 days on Earth! At 480°C, Venus is hotter than Mercury.

A year is how long it takes a planet to orbit the Sun.

A day is how long it takes a planet to rotate once on its axis.

One year on Earth takes 365 days.

One day on Mars takes just over 24 hours. A year on Mars takes 687 Earth days.

MARS

This rocky, mountainous planet has two moons: Phobos and Deimos. Iron minerals in its soil and atmosphere make it appear red. Scientists are working to determine whether Mars has ever supported life – or might do so in the future.

ASTEROID BELT

Located between the orbits of Mars and Jupiter, this region contains most of the asteroids in the solar system.

SATURN

This gas giant has at least 53 moons and seven rings, which are only about 10 metres thick. High winds – five times the speed of those on Earth – give Saturn its gold and yellow bands.
Its largest moon, Titan, is bigger than the planet Mercury.

JUPITER

This gas giant is the solar system's largest planet and contains twice the material of all the other planets combined! It has 50 moons, including Ganymede, the largest in the solar system.

A Jupiter year is 12 Earth years. It spins fast – once every 10 hours – which creates high winds. Its 'red spot' is an enormous storm twice the width of Earth that has been raging for more than 300 years.

URANUS

This ice giant has 13 rings and spins on its side, in an anticlockwise motion similar to Venus.

Neptune, also an ice giant, was predicted to exist by astronomers before it could even be seen. Due to its elliptical orbit, at some points it is further from the Sun than the dwarf planet, Pluto.

NEPTUNE

A Uranus year takes 84 Earth years. Its poles experience long dark winters lasting more than 20 years.

A Neptune year is 165 Earth years.

THE KUIPER BELT

The Kuiper Belt is located just outside Neptune's orbit. Pluto, along with most of the short-period comets, is found here.

33

IF THE PLANETS WERE FRUITS...

This is how our planets would compare
in size if they were pieces of fruit.

**VENUS =
GRAPE**
Diameter:
7,521 miles

**JUPITER =
WATERMELON**
Diameter:
88,846 miles

**MERCURY =
PEPPERCORN**
Diameter:
3,032 miles

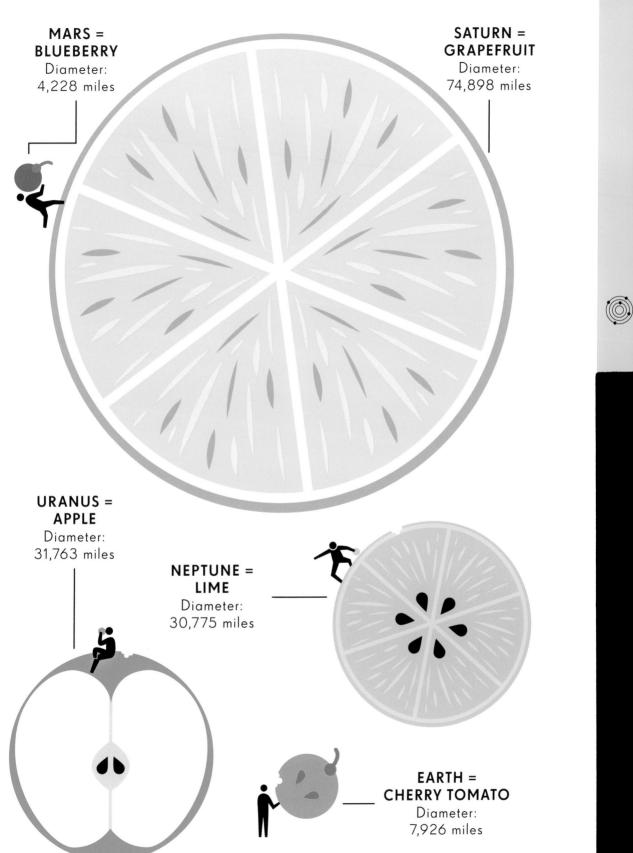

**MARS =
BLUEBERRY**
Diameter:
4,228 miles

**SATURN =
GRAPEFRUIT**
Diameter:
74,898 miles

**URANUS =
APPLE**
Diameter:
31,763 miles

**NEPTUNE =
LIME**
Diameter:
30,775 miles

**EARTH =
CHERRY TOMATO**
Diameter:
7,926 miles

WHAT ELSE IS IN THE SOLAR SYSTEM?

SNOW FLURRY

Comets are flying snowballs made of frozen rock, ice and dust. As a comet travels through space and nears the Sun, it warms up and develops a hazy atmosphere, or 'coma' and sometimes emits a vaporous tail behind it.

CELESTIAL BODY

Asteroids are small, irregularly-shaped bodies made of rock and metal. They can have a small number of moons, but no atmosphere or rings. They form closer to the Sun than comets do.

ON THE ROCKS

All meteors and meteorites start life as meteoroids: small bodies of rock and debris flying through space.

SHOOTING STAR

Meteors, also known as shooting stars, are meteoroids that have entered Earth's atmosphere and emit a spectacular flare as they burn up in just a few seconds, leaving a dusty trail behind them.

EARTH

DEEP IMPACT

Some larger meteorites have caused wide-spread devastation on Earth. Scientists think that 65 million years ago, a six-mile-wide meteorite hit what is now known as Mexico, creating a crater 110 miles wide in an explosion more powerful than one billion man-made atom bombs and causing a mass-extinction event on Earth that killed the dinosaurs.

COMET

One of the best-known comets is Halley's Comet, which is visible roughly every 75 years and is depicted in the Bayeux Tapestry.

ASTEROID

The biggest asteroid is called Ceres. It is so big that it is classed as a dwarf planet.

METEOROID

METEOR

METEORITE

DOWN TO EARTH

Made of iron and stone, meteorites are the surviving bits of meteoroids that pass through Earth's atmosphere and hit the ground at high speeds.

More than 50,000 meteorites have been found on Earth. Most are smaller than a human fist.

THE SUN

The Sun is more than just the big ball of light in the sky that gives our planet heat, and helps us to live. It is in fact a 4.5-billion-year-old yellow dwarf star, that holds us all in orbit around it with its gravitational pull.

Consisting of a core that is 15 million°C, a radio-active zone of gamma rays, and a convective zone which comprises its outer shell, the Sun makes up 99% of the solar system's mass. Something this big and hot creates a huge amount of energy through the nuclear fusion of hydrogen into helium in its core.

The Sun isn't as perfectly smooth as it may appear; its surface experiences sun spots, caused by intense magnetic activity, and solar flares, eruptions of intense high-energy radiation that shoot out of its surface. Both of these phenomena can be seen using powerful telescopes.

The Sun is the key to life on Earth, and its beautiful light-shows around the North and South Poles are just a glimpse into the amazing power held within it. But there's so much more beneath its surface...

THE SUN

At 4.5 billion years old, the Sun is a middle-aged star called a yellow dwarf.

The Sun is the star at the centre of our solar system. It is a ball of brightly burning gas, 865,000 miles wide, held together by its own gravity. It contains 99% of the mass of the entire solar system.

CHARACTERISTIC MARKS

SUN SPOTS

These temporary spots are created by intense magnetic activity, which reduces the temperature of an area and makes it visibly darker than its surroundings. They usually appear as pairs that have a north and south magnetic field.

SOLAR FLARES

Bright solar flares shoot out from the Sun's surface and release energy during magnetic storms.

GRANULATION

The mottled appearance of the Sun's surface is known as granulation and is caused by currents of heat in the convective zone.

SUN SIZE

Check out the size of the Sun in comparison to the eight planets orbiting around it!

Mercury

Venus

Earth

Mars

Jupiter

Uranus

Neptune

Saturn

The Sun has layers like an onion.

INTERNAL PARTS OF THE SUN

CORE
The core makes up about 25% of the Sun. It is where nuclear reactions consume hydrogen gases and create helium, releasing vast quantities of energy in the process in the form of gamma rays. The temperature here is about 15 million °C.

RADIOACTIVE ZONE
Gamma rays radiating from the core take hundreds of thousands of years to pass through this region because they bounce off so many other particles on their indirect path out.

CONVECTIVE ZONE
Forming the Sun's outer shell, this area looks as though it is boiling as it transfers energy to the Sun's atmosphere in the form of heat. At its surface, its temperature is about 5,000°C.

SUN'S ATMOSPHERE

PHOTOSPHERE
This is the only part of the Sun visible to the naked eye, because here, the Sun's energy is released into space as light.

CHROMOSPHERE
This thin layer sits above the photosphere and can only be seen during a solar eclipse, when it appears as a red ring around the Sun.

CORONA
Situated above the chromosphere, the pearly glow of these extremely hot gases in the Sun's corona can be seen only during a solar eclipse.

SOLAR POWER

The Sun is a giant power station, producing energy through the process of nuclear fusion. It is made up of approximately 70% hydrogen, 28% helium and 2% other gases, but these percentages are changing over time as the Sun converts hydrogen to helium.

HOW DOES THE SUN BURN?

Like all stars, the Sun creates its energy in a reaction called nuclear fusion.

This is how it works:

1. The Sun's gravity pulls its mass inwards, creating huge pressure.

CORE OF THE MATTER

Conditions at the Sun's centre are unimaginably hot and dense.

The **temperature** is 15 million°C.

The **pressure** is 250 billion times more than Earth's atmosphere at sea level.

The **density** is 150 times more than that of water.

2. The hot temperatures and high pressure act on the hydrogen atoms, causing them to fuse together, creating helium.

4. The energy produced by fusion is released as heat and radiation.

3. Fusion converts part of the mass to energy.

GREAT WATT

The Sun's power is 386 billion mega watts, equivalent to nearly 7,000 trillion 60-watt light bulbs!

EXCHANGE RATE

Every second, 700 million tons of hydrogen are converted into about 695 million tons of helium and 5 million tons of energy in the form of gamma rays.

STAR ATTRACTION

The convection currents around the Sun create a huge magnetic field, which extends far out into space, even beyond Pluto. Earth has its own magnetic field, caused by the movement of molten lava, which protects us from most of the harmful radiation that hits us from space.

WINDFALL

Solar winds, also known as solar plasma, are streams of hot, charged gas particles that are emitted from the Sun through holes in its corona.

CATCHING RAYS

Solar flares launch charged particles, X-rays and other radiation towards Earth. These particles shake up the magnetosphere and can disable satellites.

FLARE UP

The Sun repeats a cycle roughly every 11 years. During the cycle, activity around the Sun increases, sun spots appear, solar storms erupt, solar flares become more common, and its magnetic field flips.

WEAK POINT

Earth's magnetic shield is weakest at the poles, allowing particles to enter Earth's atmosphere, where they interfere with the navigation systems of any aircraft in their path.

MAGNETIC FIELD

NORTH POLE

SOUTH POLE

MAGNETIC SHIELD

CHARGED UP

When charged particles in the solar winds enter Earth's atmosphere and collide with oxygen and nitrogen atoms, they release flashes of coloured light.

These light-shows appear around Earth's magnetic poles. In the North, they are known as the Aurora Borealis, and in the South Pole, they are called the Aurora Australis.

THE EARTH AND MOON

As far as we know, Earth is the only planet in the Universe to sustain life. It is situated the perfect distance away from the Sun, so it's never too hot or too cold, and a magnetic field protects it from solar radiation.

Covered mostly in water, it contains a core of iron and nickel so dense that it never melts, even at its temperature of 6,000°C. Surrounded by an atmosphere that burns up meteors and is filled with gases that allow us to breathe, Earth is very good at making sure that life on its surface is protected. In addition, Earth's rotation and orbit determines our calendars.

Having one moon that orbits around us gives us a glimpse into the wider Universe. The Moon is the only planetary body that humankind has set foot on besides our own. The Moon's gravity affects our tides, and it can be seen by the reflection of the Sun's light. When the Moon, Earth and the Sun align in certain ways, we get amazing eclipses.

You might think you know a lot about the planet you live on, but do you really? Explore even more, and find out just what makes up the rock beneath your feet.

HABITABLE EARTH

Earth was created about 4.5 billion years ago, along with the rest of the solar system. It is the only planet in the Universe known to sustain life.

Radius 5-70 km thick ➤

ON TOP OF THE WORLD

The crust is Earth's outermost layer. It is divided into tectonic plates that float on the mantle and slowly move a few centimetres per year, causing earthquakes and volcanic eruptions as they shift.

Up to 2,890 km thick ➤

MOVING MOUNTAINS

Most of the Earth's internal heat is stored in the mantle. Convective currents in the molten upper mantle create movement in Earth's crust, which floats above it.

Up to 2,300 km thick ▬

ON THE RISE

The fluid molten outer core experiences movement due to convection, which causes the hotter fluid to rise and colder material to sink. This process is thought to create Earth's protective magnetic field.

Up to 1,250 km thick ▬

HEAVY HEART

Earth is the densest planet in the Universe, thanks to its inner core, which is made mostly of iron and some nickel. Earth's density is so high that even at temperatures of 6,000°C, its core remains solid.

STRUCTURE OF EARTH

CRUST

MANTLE

OUTER CORE

INNER CORE

BLUE PLANET

About 71% of Earth is covered by water. It is the only known planet with large amounts of liquid water.

WHAT MAKES EARTH HABITABLE?

LOCATION, LOCATION

Its distance from the Sun means it's not too close and hot, and not too far and cold.

HAVE A FIELD DAY

Its magnetic field protects it from harmful solar radiation.

BUBBLE WRAP

Its atmosphere keeps it at the right temperature, and protects it from meteors.

GOOD CHEMISTRY

It has the right chemical balance, which allows for breathable air, liquid water and rich mineral and energy resources.

LEASE OF LIFE

Earth's temperate climate allows water to exist in liquid form – which is crucial in supporting life.

EARTH'S ATMOSPHERE

Earth's atmosphere extends about 620 miles into space, and gets thinner the further from Earth's centre you travel.

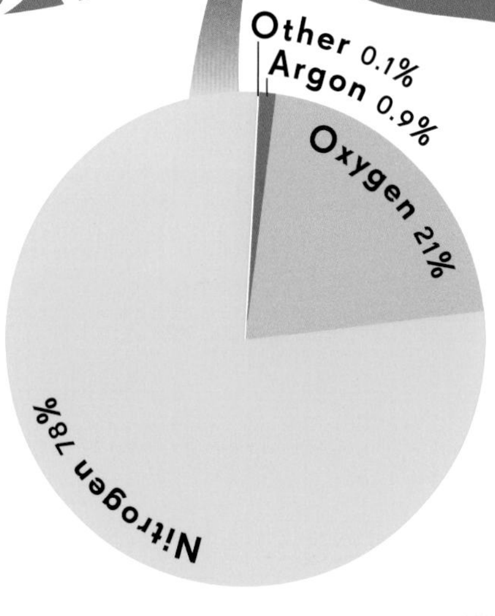

Other 0.1%
Argon 0.9%
Oxygen 21%
Nitrogen 78%

Noctilucent Clouds

These luminous clouds are seen at night in summer, in high altitudes.

BREATH OF LIFE

Many planets have an atmosphere, but only Earth's atmosphere contains air that can sustain life. This is due to its balance of gases.

Satellite

620 miles

EXOSPHERE

GREENHOUSE EFFECT

Earth is wrapped in a layer of gases called the atmosphere. This layer acts like a greenhouse, allowing the Sun's heat to pass through and then trapping it in, keeping Earth warm, even at night, when the Sun's rays are blocked.

Spacecraft

THERMOSPHERE
100 miles

MESOPAUSE
75 miles

MESOSPHERE
50 miles

Meteors

SHIELD

As meteors pass through the atmosphere at high speeds, the gases cause them to burn up completely. In this way, the atmosphere acts as a protective shield to life on Earth.

STRATOSPHERE
25 miles

FAIR-WEATHER FRIEND

The circulation of atmospheric gases distributes heat and water vapour around Earth and creates climate systems. These weather patterns bring winds, rains and constant temperatures that allow plants to grow and animals to survive.

Radiosonde
This mini weather station measures pressure, temperature and humidity.

The ozone layer filters out harmful radiation from space.

OZONE

Commercial planes

Mount Everest

Passenger hot-air balloons

TROPOSPHERE

EARTH'S CALENDAR

A year on Earth is divided into four seasons. In the northern hemisphere, the seasons look like this...

YEARLY CYCLE One year on Earth is measured according to the time it takes to complete one orbit of the Sun: 365.25 days.

LEAP YEAR To account for the quarter days, we have three years that are 365 days long. Every fourth year, the four quarter days add one extra day to the calendar year, giving us a leap year of 366 days.

AUTUMN

WINTER Earth has completed half of its orbit months after summer, when the northern hemisphere is tilted away from the Sun, experiences shorter days, and experiences winter.

12 MONTHS One month on Earth roughly corresponds to one complete phase from a new moon to a full moon and back again. This happens approximately 12 times each year.

DAY AND NIGHT

As it travels around the Sun, Earth spins on its axis. One complete rotation takes 24 hours and takes Earth through one complete cycle from day to night and back to day.

52

SUMMER DOWN UNDER

Even though they are relatively close geographically, because they are situated in opposite hemispheres, Australia has its summer when it's winter in Japan!

ON THE TILT Earth has seasons because its axis is tilted. It rotates on its axis as it orbits the Sun, but the axis always points in the same direction. Earth spins on an axis of 23.45 degrees. This means that as it moves around the Sun during the course of the year, different parts of Earth tilt towards the Sun and receive more of its light.

BRIGHT NIGHTS During the northern hemisphere's summer, its tip — the North Pole — receives light from the Sun the entire time that it spins, so it is light for a full 24-hour period.

DARK DAYS Conversely, when it's summer in the northern hemisphere, the southern hemisphere experiences winter and 24-hour periods of darkness at the South Pole.

SUMMER

When the northern hemisphere is tilted towards the Sun, it has longer days, brighter nights and experiences summer.

SPRING

The areas lit by the Sun experience day.

The areas facing away from the Sun experience night.

53

THE MOON

The Moon is the only body in space beyond Earth to have been visited by humankind.

BUMPY START

Scientists think the Moon was created when a Mars-size body collided with the young Earth 4.5 billion years ago.

CLOUDY SKIES

The collision sent huge quantities of dust and debris into space, which began to orbit Earth.

GATHERING DUST

Under Earth's force of attraction, the rock fragments continued to circle around our planet, eventually joining together to form the Moon.

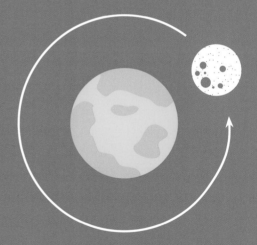

THE BRIGHT SIDE

The Moon orbits Earth once every 27.3 days and takes exactly the same period of time to spin on its axis, which means that we always see the same face of the Moon.

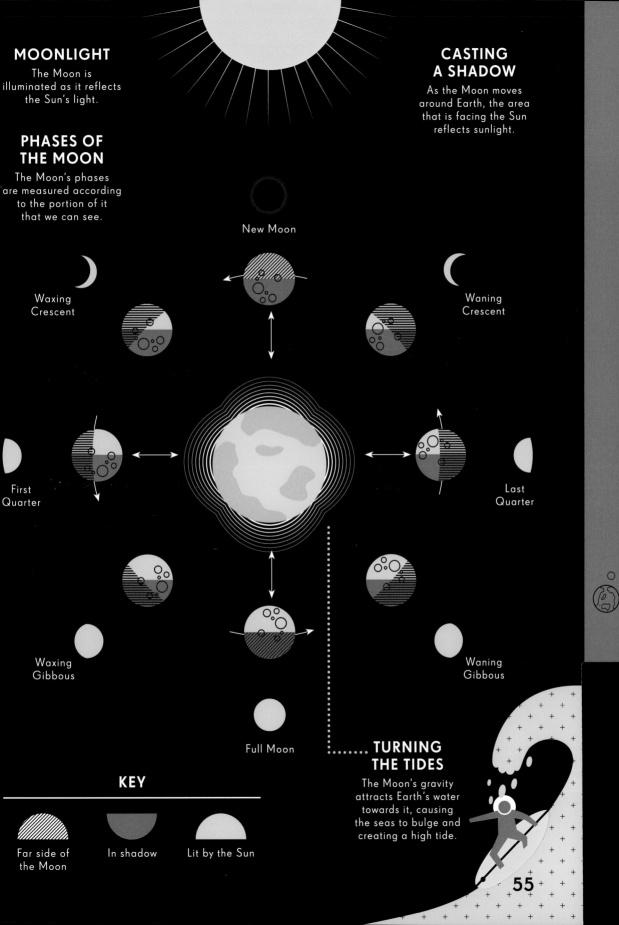

MOONLIGHT
The Moon is illuminated as it reflects the Sun's light.

CASTING A SHADOW
As the Moon moves around Earth, the area that is facing the Sun reflects sunlight.

PHASES OF THE MOON
The Moon's phases are measured according to the portion of it that we can see.

New Moon

Waxing Crescent

Waning Crescent

First Quarter

Last Quarter

Waxing Gibbous

Waning Gibbous

Full Moon

TURNING THE TIDES
The Moon's gravity attracts Earth's water towards it, causing the seas to bulge and creating a high tide.

KEY

Far side of the Moon

In shadow

Lit by the Sun

ECLIPSES

The Sun's distance from Earth is approximately 400 times that of the Moon. The Sun is also approximately 400 times the diameter of the Moon. This means that from Earth, the Sun and Moon appear to be approximately the same size.

MOON'S ORBIT

PARTIAL SOLAR ECLIPSE

TOTAL SOLAR ECLIPSE

How the Sun looks from Earth

THE SHADOWS

Occasionally, when the orbital positions are right, the Moon can block and prevent the Sun's light from reaching Earth and vice versa. This is known as an eclipse.

SOLAR ECLIPSE

A total solar eclipse occurs when the Moon passes between Earth and the Sun, completely blocking the Sun's light. When this happens, the Sun disappears from view and all that is visible is its glowing atmosphere – its corona – which seems to surround the Moon in a white halo. For a few minutes, Earth falls into darkness.

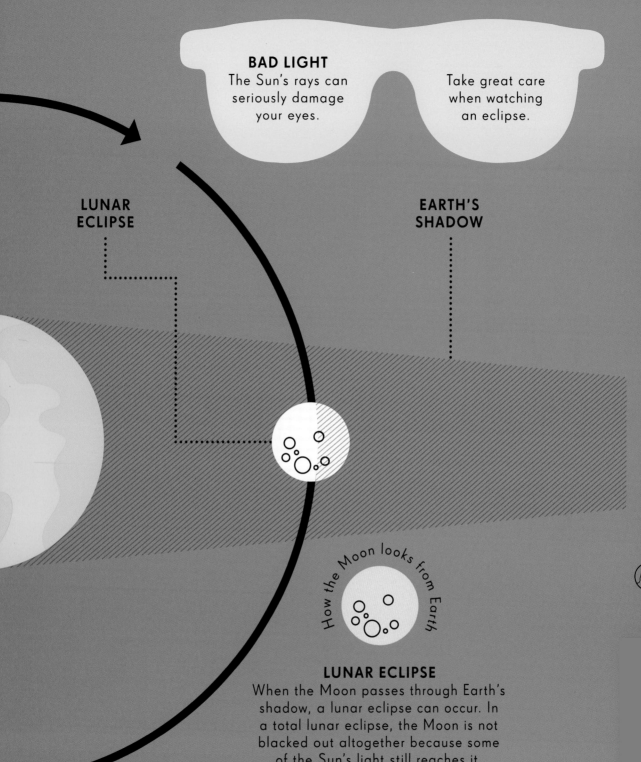

BAD LIGHT
The Sun's rays can seriously damage your eyes.

Take great care when watching an eclipse.

LUNAR ECLIPSE

EARTH'S SHADOW

How the Moon looks from Earth

LUNAR ECLIPSE

When the Moon passes through Earth's shadow, a lunar eclipse can occur. In a total lunar eclipse, the Moon is not blacked out altogether because some of the Sun's light still reaches it, refracted (bent) around Earth. As this sunlight passes through the Earth's atmosphere, the blue coloured light is filtered out. The remaining light causes the Moon to appear red.

OBSERVING SPACE

For as long as we have gazed up at the stars in the night sky, physicists and astronomers have studied space to try to unravel the mysterious workings of the Universe. Closer observation of space was made possible with the invention of the telescope. As far back as the 17th century, Galileo used an optical telescope to support the theory put forward earlier by Copernicus, that the Sun is at the centre of our solar system. There are now several different types of telescope, with different uses.

For centuries, observing the stars has been essential for navigation purposes. In the southern hemisphere, travellers use the Southern Cross and the Pointer stars to determine their location, while in the northern hemisphere, the North Star, or Polaris, points travellers due north.

To get closer to the stars and deeper into our galaxy, scientists have sent probes and rovers into space to explore the planets in our solar system. They can get up close and personal with a planet's surface, and report their findings back to Earth.

Astronomers, physicists and other scientists can all put together an amazing picture of what lies in outer space. Perhaps one day we will discover that we are not alone...

FAMOUS NAMES IN ASTRONOMY

NICOLAUS COPERNICUS

Thorn, Poland (1473–1543)

aka the 'Father of Modern Astronomy'

Optical telescopes cannot be used in bad weather conditions.

Copernicus formulated a heliocentric model of our solar system, placing the Sun, rather than Earth, at its centre.

MODERN OPTICAL TELESCOPES

Viewing a faraway object

Light rays

Viewing the same object through a telescope

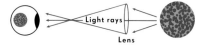

Light rays

Lens

Optical telescopes enhance the human eye, magnifying the visible light from space. They work in a similar way to a magnifying glass – a lens or mirror collects lots of light and focuses it. Then a second lens 'spreads out' the focused light and makes it appear larger.

Pisa, Italy (1564–1642)
GALILEO GALILEI
aka the 'Father
of Modern Science'

Galileo used an optical telescope to study the planets. He defended Copernicus's heliocentric model, and discovered the four largest moons of Jupiter and the rings of Saturn.

Lincolnshire, England (1643–1727)
SIR ISAAC NEWTON

Missouri, USA
(1889–1953)
EDWIN HUBBLE

Hubble made observations that supported the theory of an expanding Universe. Hubble's law indicates that the further away an astronomical object is, the faster it is travelling away from the viewer.

Oxford, England
(1942–)
**STEPHEN
HAWKING**

Newton was a busy man! He devised the reflecting telescope, using a mirror instead of a lens; he came up with the three laws of motion – inertia, acceleration, action/reaction – and he worked out the laws of gravitational force!

Hawking has contributed groundbreaking studies of black holes and their relationship to the origin of the Universe.

61

STUDYING THE STARS

· ·

Telescopes allow us to understand the structure and evolution of the Universe. Bigger, more powerful telescopes give deeper and more detailed views of the Universe. Launched into space, they record information that gets relayed back to Earth.

X-RAY TELESCOPES

X-ray telescopes collect the X-rays emitted from the Sun, stars and supernovas in space. They operate in high altitude, where the atmosphere is thinner.

Launched in 1999, Chandra X-Ray Observatory is the world's most powerful X-ray telescope.

HUBBLE SPACE TELESCOPE

Named after Edwin Hubble, and launched in 1990, the Hubble Space Telescope was the first major optical telescope placed in space above Earth's atmosphere for an undistorted view.

Hubble is the size of a large school bus. It weighs as much as two adult elephants!

RADIO TELESCOPES

Objects in space can be noisy! Radio telescopes detect noise from radio wavelengths and convert this noise into a picture of the object making it.

Launched in 2011, Russia's RadioAstron Observatory is the biggest radio telescope in space. Its antenna is 10 metres in diameter.

The James Webb Infrared Space Telescope is designed to study every phase in the history of our Universe. Scheduled to launch in 2018, it is 7 times more powerful than the Hubble telescope.

INFRARED TELESCOPES

Infrared radiation is heat energy emitted from objects. Objects that do not emit enough light to be seen using the naked eye or an optical telescope can be observed using an Infrared Astronomical Satellite (IRAS).

LENS SIZE COMPARISON

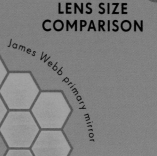

James Webb primary mirror

Hubble primary mirror

USING THE STARS & CONSTELLATIONS

For thousands of years, travellers have used stars to navigate, as the constellations are constant landmarks. They appear to move as Earth rotates, but their positions to other stars never change.

THE SOUTHERN HEMISPHERE

SOUTHERN CROSS

SOUTH CELESTIAL POLE

POINTER STARS

ACHERNAR

SOUTH

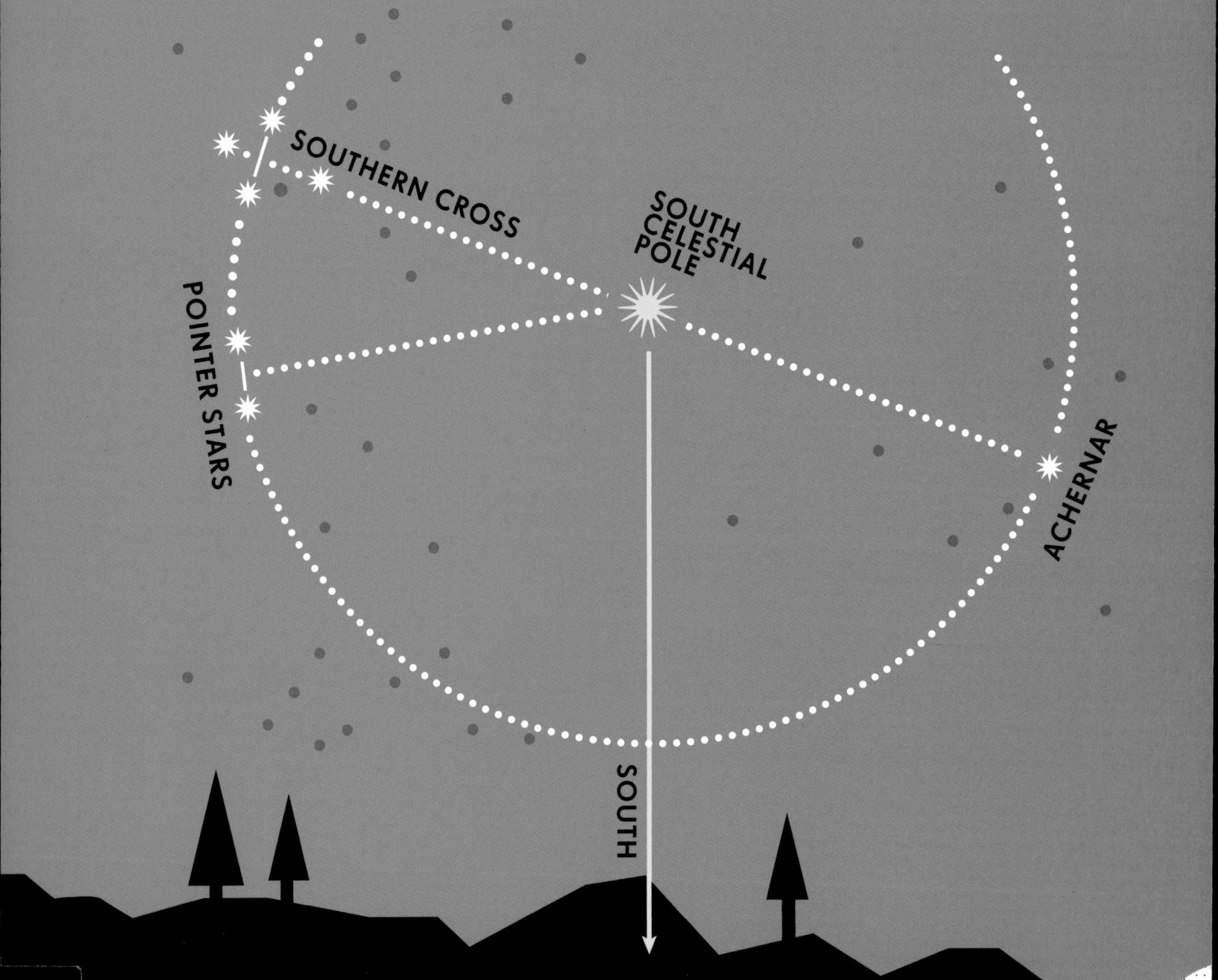

In the southern hemisphere, look for the Southern Cross and the two Pointer stars. Picture them at the rim of a circle, as shown here. Then imagine lines through each of them at 90-degree angles to the circle's edge. Where the lines intersect indicates due south.

THE PLOUGH or BIG DIPPER

The Plough or Big Dipper is formed by the seven brightest stars of Ursa Major, the Great Bear.

LITTLE DIPPER

The North Star, or Polaris, is the tip of the Little Dipper's handle, and the brightest star in Ursa Minor.

CASSIOPEIA

Cassiopeia is named after a vain queen in Greek mythology. She sits upside down on her throne, with her head pointing towards Polaris.

THE NORTHERN HEMISPHERE

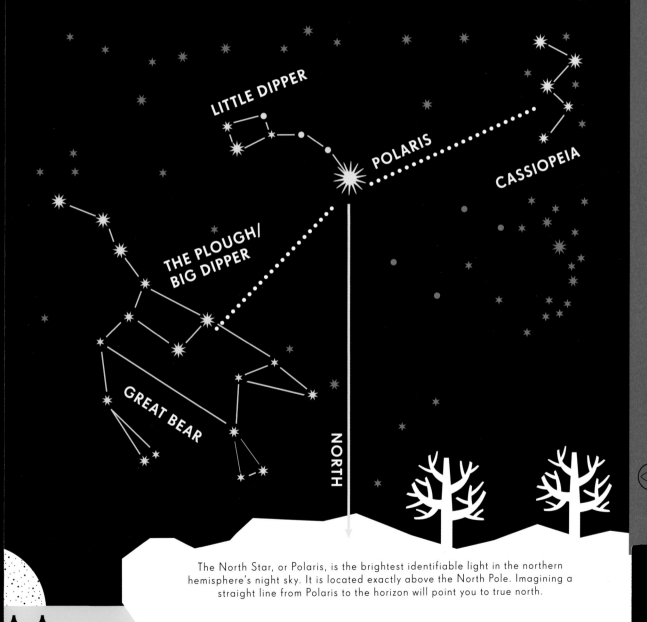

LITTLE DIPPER

POLARIS

CASSIOPEIA

THE PLOUGH/ BIG DIPPER

GREAT BEAR

NORTH

The North Star, or Polaris, is the brightest identifiable light in the northern hemisphere's night sky. It is located exactly above the North Pole. Imagining a straight line from Polaris to the horizon will point you to true north.

ROVERS & PROBES

Space probes are unmanned. They either orbit planets to collect data and images, or they land on other planets and take samples so that scientists back on Earth can learn more about conditions such as weather, toxins and gravity.

Rovers are robotic vehicles that can land on a planet, explore its surface, collect data, and take pictures.

Four rovers have landed on Mars – look how far they've travelled across its surface!

SOJOURNER
1997
0.06 miles

SPIRIT
2004–2010
4.8 miles

CURIOSITY
2012–Present
5.3 miles

OPPORTUNITY
2004–Present
25 miles

The first probe was Sputnik 1, launched on October 4th 1957. It studied Earth from space.

Launched in 1977, Voyager 1 has travelled further than any other man-made object in space. As of 2013 it registered at 11.6 billion miles from Earth.

ARE WE ALONE?

Some scientists think that life on Earth might have come from Mars! A particular form of the element molybdenum may have been important in the creation of life, but isn't likely to have existed on Earth at the time life began here. It might, however, have existed on Mars and been brought to Earth in a meteorite. So we could all be Martians.

EXPLORING SPACE

Humankind's unquenchable curiosity has led to exploration and discovery that have brought about amazing advances in space technology. From the first human space flight in 1961, which took Yuri Gagarin into orbit around Earth, to the launch of the live-in International Space Station in 1988, space exploration continues and groundbreaking discoveries are made.

Follow the path of Apollo 11, which successfully landed man on the Moon in 1969, then blast off in the space shuttle – but don't forget your spacesuit or you won't survive for long!

A variety of animals have also been rocketed into space. The first were fruit flies back in 1947, sent to measure the effects of radiation exposure in high altitudes. Dogs, cats, monkeys and even spiders have all played their part in exploring the unknown.

Did you know that the crew of the International Space Station live in space for 6–12 months at a time? They experience several sunrises a day, as the space station orbits Earth over and over again!

THE GIANT LEAP

In 1969, Apollo 11 was the first spaceflight to successfully land a person on the Moon. Neil Armstrong and Buzz Aldrin spent 21 hours on lunar soil, conducting experiments and taking photographs and samples. The third astronaut, Michael Collins, remained in lunar orbit.

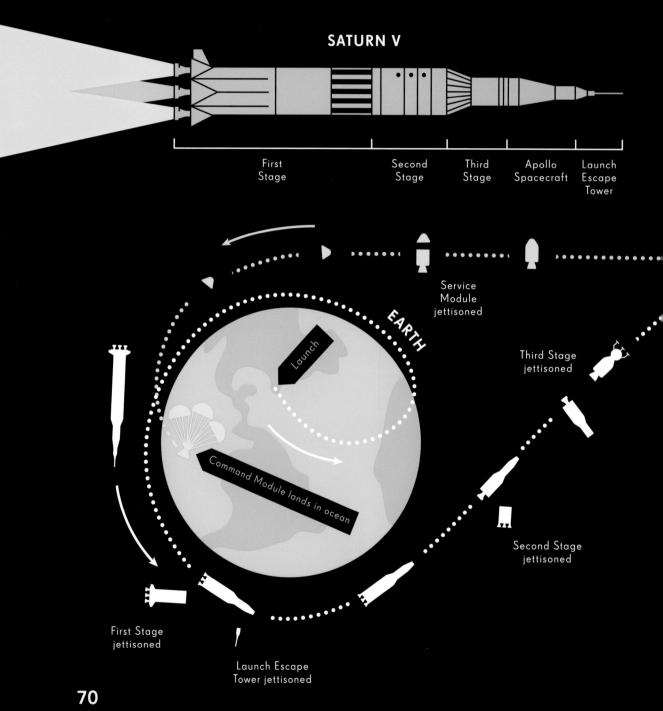

SATURN V

First Stage

Second Stage

Third Stage

Apollo Spacecraft

Launch Escape Tower

Service Module jettisoned

Third Stage jettisoned

EARTH

Launch

Command Module lands in ocean

Second Stage jettisoned

First Stage jettisoned

Launch Escape Tower jettisoned

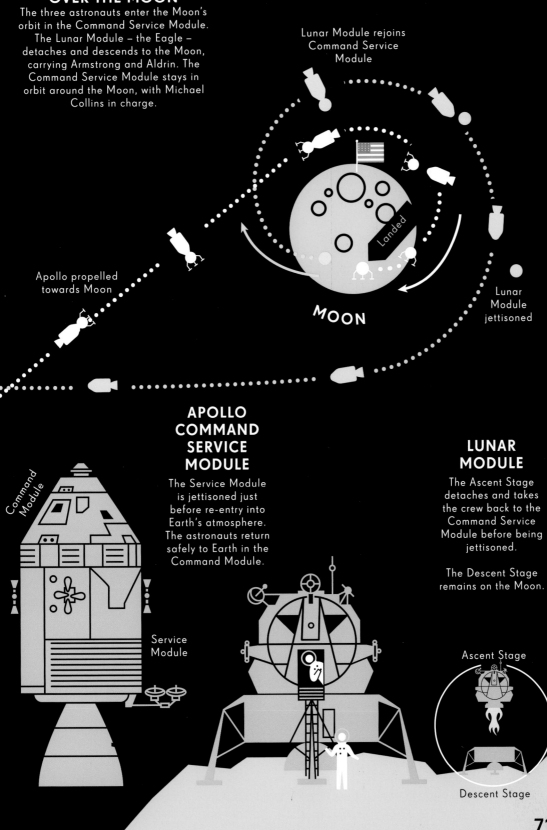

OVER THE MOON

The three astronauts enter the Moon's orbit in the Command Service Module. The Lunar Module – the Eagle – detaches and descends to the Moon, carrying Armstrong and Aldrin. The Command Service Module stays in orbit around the Moon, with Michael Collins in charge.

Lunar Module rejoins Command Service Module

Apollo propelled towards Moon

Landed

MOON

Lunar Module jettisoned

APOLLO COMMAND SERVICE MODULE

The Service Module is jettisoned just before re-entry into Earth's atmosphere. The astronauts return safely to Earth in the Command Module.

Command Module

Service Module

LUNAR MODULE

The Ascent Stage detaches and takes the crew back to the Command Service Module before being jettisoned.

The Descent Stage remains on the Moon.

Ascent Stage

Descent Stage

LAUNCHING INTO SPACE

Rockets are the engines that blast probes, satellites and shuttles into space. The space shuttle is launched into orbit by rocket engines, then lands back on Earth like an aeroplane. It is designed to be re-used.

LIFT OFF
The solid rocket boosters and shuttle main engines generate enough thrust for blast off.

ROCKET SEPARATION
Their fuel used up after 2 minutes, the booster rockets detach.

ROCKET DESCENT
The boosters parachute into the ocean, for recovery and re-use.

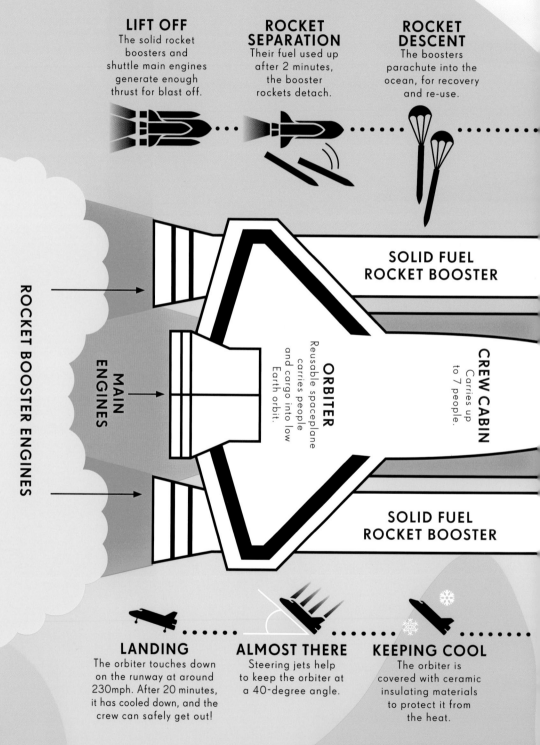

ROCKET BOOSTER ENGINES

MAIN ENGINES

ORBITER
Reusable spaceplane carries people and cargo into low Earth orbit.

CREW CABIN
Carries up to 7 people.

SOLID FUEL ROCKET BOOSTER

SOLID FUEL ROCKET BOOSTER

LANDING
The orbiter touches down on the runway at around 230mph. After 20 minutes, it has cooled down, and the crew can safely get out!

ALMOST THERE
Steering jets help to keep the orbiter at a 40-degree angle.

KEEPING COOL
The orbiter is covered with ceramic insulating materials to protect it from the heat.

72

WHICH COUNTRIES HAVE ROCKETED INTO SPACE?

France

United States

Russia

China

Iran

Japan

Israel

North Korea

India

TANK JETTISON

The external tank falls to Earth when its fuel is used up. It burns up in Earth's atmosphere over the ocean.

IN ORBIT

Just 8.5 minutes after take-off, small rocket engines fire the shuttle into orbit.

ROCKET NOSE

The frame of a rocket is very strong. A rocket's nose cone often carries what is referred to as the payload. The payload's components are dependent on the mission of the rocket.

EXTERNAL TANK

Carries fuel and oxygen for the main engines.

TAIL-FIRST

To prepare for re-entry, thrusters turn the orbiter upside down. It now travels tail-first to slow its speed.

HEATING UP

Travelling at 17,000 mph, the orbiter builds up heat from friction with air molecules. Temperatures reach 1,650°C.

UPPER ATMOSPHERE

After about 25 minutes, the orbiter reaches the upper atmosphere. Thrusters are fired to turn the orbiter over, so it is moving nose-first again.

SURVIVAL IN SPACE

Spacesuits are like a small, personal spacecraft. They are constructed from many different components, and protect astronauts from the dangerous environment of space.

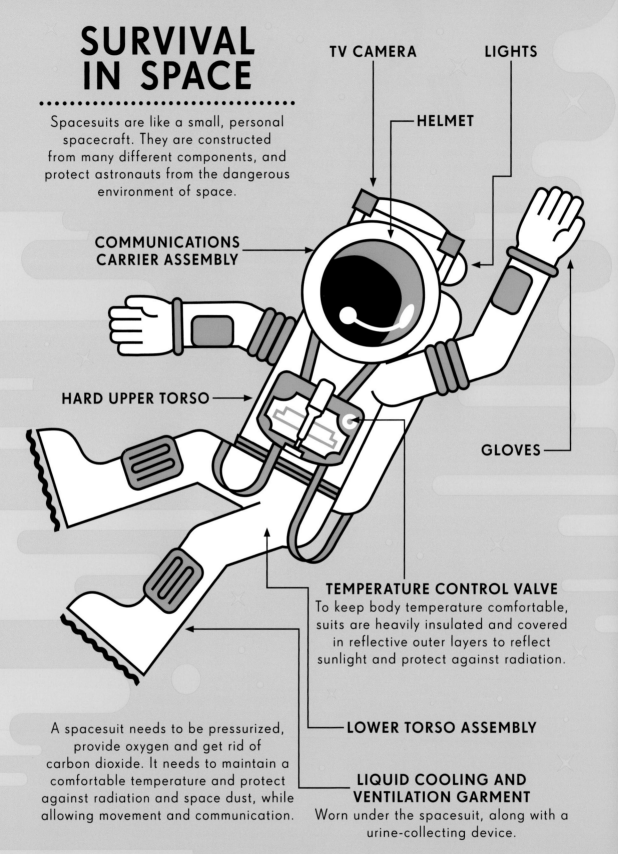

TV CAMERA

LIGHTS

HELMET

COMMUNICATIONS CARRIER ASSEMBLY

HARD UPPER TORSO

GLOVES

TEMPERATURE CONTROL VALVE
To keep body temperature comfortable, suits are heavily insulated and covered in reflective outer layers to reflect sunlight and protect against radiation.

LOWER TORSO ASSEMBLY

A spacesuit needs to be pressurized, provide oxygen and get rid of carbon dioxide. It needs to maintain a comfortable temperature and protect against radiation and space dust, while allowing movement and communication.

LIQUID COOLING AND VENTILATION GARMENT
Worn under the spacesuit, along with a urine-collecting device.

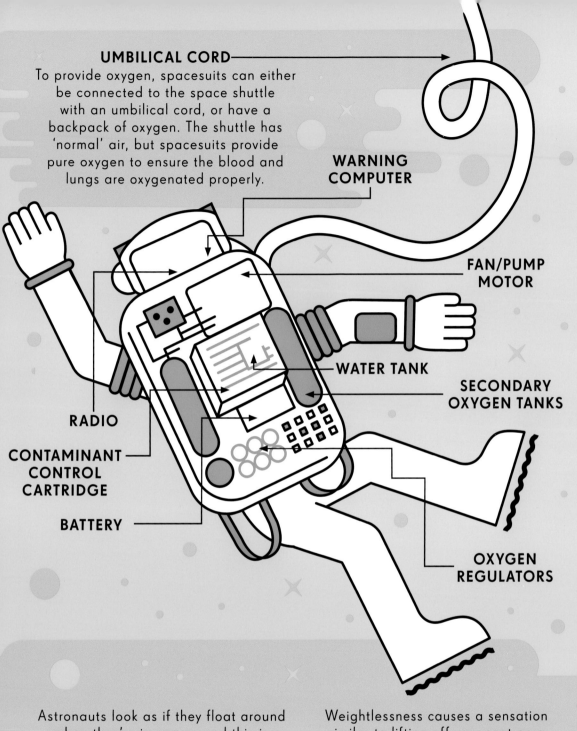

UMBILICAL CORD

To provide oxygen, spacesuits can either be connected to the space shuttle with an umbilical cord, or have a backpack of oxygen. The shuttle has 'normal' air, but spacesuits provide pure oxygen to ensure the blood and lungs are oxygenated properly.

WARNING COMPUTER

FAN/PUMP MOTOR

WATER TANK

SECONDARY OXYGEN TANKS

RADIO

CONTAMINANT CONTROL CARTRIDGE

BATTERY

OXYGEN REGULATORS

Astronauts look as if they float around when they're in space, and this is because there is less gravity the further away from Earth you travel. Your mass stays the same, but your weight can change depending on the strength of the gravitational pull.

Weightlessness causes a sensation similar to lifting off your seat on a roller coaster, or missing a step walking down the stairs. Astronauts in orbit are actually falling towards Earth, but the velocity of the spacecraft keeps them in orbital motion.

ANIMALS AND ASTRONAUTS

FEBRUARY 1947
The first animals sent into space were **fruit flies**. The purpose of the experiment was to explore the effects of radiation exposure at high altitudes.

JUNE 1948
Albert I, a **rhesus monkey**, was the first mammal launched into space.

SEPTEMBER 1951
Yorick, a **monkey**, and 11 **mice** landed successfully after a space flight.

JANUARY 1961
Ham, a **chimpanzee**, was trained to pull levers to receive bananas while he travelled in space.

APRIL 1961
Soviet cosmonaut **Yuri Gagarin** was the first human in space, making a 108-minute orbital flight.

MAY 1961
Alan B Shepard Jr was the first American in space.

JULY 1969
Neil Armstrong was the first person on the Moon, with **Buzz Aldrin** a close second!

NOVEMBER 1970
Two **bullfrogs** were launched on a one-way mission to learn more about the effects of prolonged weightlessness.

JULY 1973
Two **garden spiders** named Arabella and Anita were used to study how orbiting Earth would affect spiders' ability to spin webs.

JULY 1959
A Soviet rocket reached 132 miles carrying two **dogs** and Marfusa, the first **rabbit** to go into space.

AUGUST 1960
Belka and Strelka, two **dogs**, were sent up by the Soviet Union and were the first animals to orbit and return alive.

OCTOBER 1960
The USA sent 3 **mice**, Sally, Amy and Moe 621 miles up into space.

JUNE 1963
Soviet cosmonaut **Valentina Tereshkova** was the first woman in space.

OCTOBER 1963
The French launched the first **cat**. Félicette had electrodes implanted in her skin to transmit her condition.

FEBRUARY 1966
Russian **dogs** Veterok and Ugolyok orbited for a record 22 days. Their record for longest space flight by dogs still stands.

JUNE 1983
Dr. Sally Ride was the first American woman in space.

JULY 1985
Newts can grow new limbs,so scientists were able to study regeneration in space by sending them up with parts of their limbs missing.

SEPTEMBER 2007
Microscopic creatures called tardigrades, known for being able to withstand extreme conditions, survived 10 days exposed to open space.

LIVING IN SPACE

The International Space Station is a working laboratory orbiting 240 miles above Earth. It is as large as a football field and consists of a series of metal modules.

The international crew live on the Space Station from 6 months to a year.

The ISS circles Earth many times a day, so the crew enjoy lots of sunrises.

SLEEPING
Sleeping bags are attached to the wall, in tiny cabins with room for just one. The microgravity means the crew can sleep upright!

HARD AT WORK
The crew conduct scientific research, and medical experiments on the effects of living in a microgravity environment.

They also have to maintain the ISS, and keep it neat and tidy!

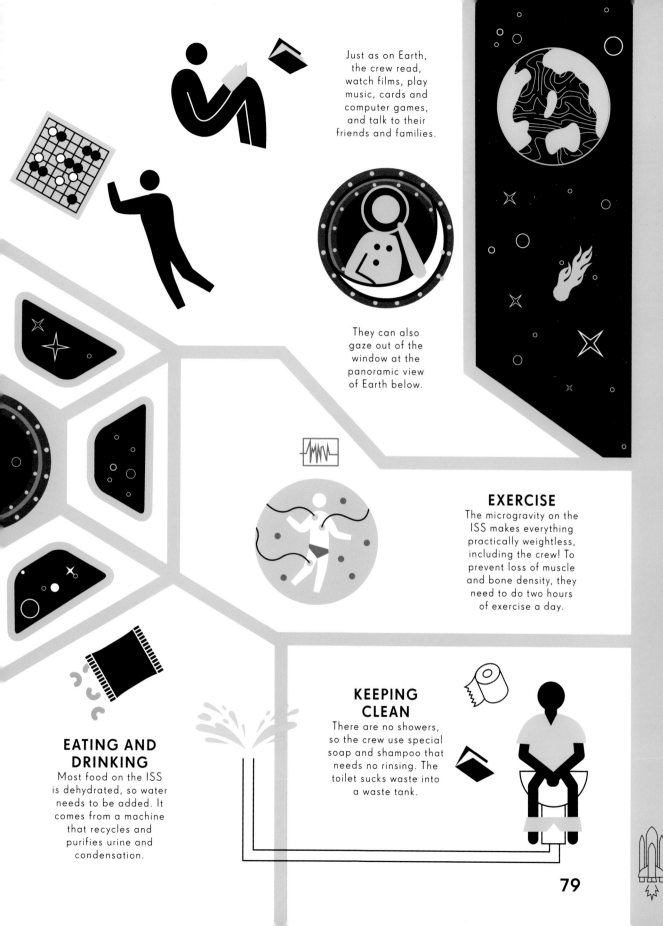

Just as on Earth, the crew read, watch films, play music, cards and computer games, and talk to their friends and families.

They can also gaze out of the window at the panoramic view of Earth below.

EXERCISE

The microgravity on the ISS makes everything practically weightless, including the crew! To prevent loss of muscle and bone density, they need to do two hours of exercise a day.

EATING AND DRINKING

Most food on the ISS is dehydrated, so water needs to be added. It comes from a machine that recycles and purifies urine and condensation.

KEEPING CLEAN

There are no showers, so the crew use special soap and shampoo that needs no rinsing. The toilet sucks waste into a waste tank.

B P P

BIG PICTURE PRESS
www.bigpicturepress.net

First published in the UK and Australia
in 2015 by Big Picture Press, part of the
Bonnier Publishing Group,
The Plaza, 535 King's Road, London,
SW10 0SZ
www.bonnierpublishing.com

ISBN 978-1-78370-143-8

Printed in China

This book was typeset in Super Grotesk
The illustrations were created digitally

Designed by Joe Hales
Design Assistant Sam Eccles

Jennifer Daniel is a visual journalist
at the New York Times where she
designs diagrams, builds interactive
graphics, and illustrates all kinds of
things including, but not limited to,
hot dogs, anthropomorphic basketballs,
and UFOs.

Simon Rogers edited and created
guardian.co.uk/data, probably the
world's most popular data journalism
website and online data resource.
Publishing hundreds of raw data sets,
it encourages its users to visualise
and analyse them. He has previously
worked at Twitter in San Francisco as the
organisation's first Data Editor.